"Crybaby, crybaby.

Mason dreaded going to school. He kicked at snow clumps in the yard. Maybe he could hide in the woods all day, then just go home at night. Maybe he could act like he'd slipped off the Black River bridge and pretend his leg was broken. Maybe it would be better to really have a broken leg than to have to be tormented by Aden.

Ira was in the yard. He held a stick in both hands, and he had Mama's tin colander on his head.

"What are you doing?" Mason asked him.

"I'm fighting the Germans. Wanna play a little while?" Ira asked. "You can wear my helmet and use my gun."

Mason cuffed Ira's head and knocked off the colander.

"Who'd want to play with you? You're just a dumb kid."

Ira's lips puckered, and he ran for the house.

"Crybaby, crybaby," Mason sang, but inside he wondered if he would ever feel worse than he did right then.

WITHDRAWN

The Night the Bells Rang

NATALIE KINSEY-WARNOCK
illustrated by LESLIE W. BOWMAN

PUFFIN BOOKS

PUFFIN BOOKS
Published by the Penguin Group
Penguin Putnam Books for Young Readers,
345 Hudson Street, New York, New York 10014, U.S.A.
Penguin Books Ltd, 27 Wrights Lane, London W8 5TZ, England
Penguin Books Australia Ltd, Ringwood, Victoria, Australia
Penguin Books Canada Ltd, 10 Alcorn Avenue, Toronto, Ontario, Canada M4V 3B2
Penguin Books (N.Z.) Ltd, 182-190 Wairau Road, Auckland 10, New Zealand

Penguin Books Ltd, Registered Offices: Harmondsworth, Middlesex, England

First published in the United States of America by Cobblehill Books, an affiliate of
Dutton Children's Books, a division of Penguin Books USA Inc., 1991
Published by Puffin Books,
a division of Penguin Putnam Books for Young Readers, 2000

1 3 5 7 9 10 8 6 4 2

THE LIBRARY OF CONGRESS HAS CATALOGED THE COBBLEHILL EDITION AS FOLLOWS:
Kinsey-Warnock, Natalie.
The night the bells rang / Natalie Kinsey-Warnock; illustrated by Leslie W. Bowman.
p. cm.
Summary: The last year of World War I is an eventful one for Vermont farm boy
Mason as he helps with the chores, tries to get along with his little brother,
and sees an older bully go off to the war.
ISBN 0-525-65074-1
[1. Vermont—Fiction. 2. Farm life—Fiction.
3. World War, 1914–1918—United States—Fiction.]
I. Bowman, Leslie W., ill. II. Title.
PZ7.K6293Ni 1991 [Fic]—dc20 91-3053 CIP AC

Puffin Books ISBN 0-14-130986-5

Printed in the United States of America

RL: 3.3

FOR MY FATHER,
FREDERICK KINSEY

The Night the Bells Rang

ONE

Stars glittered like ice in the darkness. Mason turtled his chin into the sheepskin collar of his coat, and held the lantern higher as he stumbled toward the buttery light that shone from the window. He had never felt such a biting wind. It blew out of the north, from Canada, and wrapped around him like a blanket, taking his breath away. On most nights, he would have taken a moment to look at the sky and pick out the constellations he knew. But not on a night like this. Besides, his stomach was growling; he wondered what Mama was cooking for supper.

A blast of cold air followed him into the kitchen. His mother looked up from her kneading as the wind picked up snow from the ground and swirled it through the room.

"Your father coming in soon?" she asked. Bits of bread dough clung to her fingers, and there was a smudge of flour on her nose.

Mason stamped off his boots and set the lantern on the table.

"He'll be in, in a minute," he said. "He wanted to check Chelsea."

"This cold goes right to a body's bones," Mama said. "Would be a bad night for that foal to be born. Seems as babies only come on bad nights, though." She smiled at Mason. "You did." Then she changed the subject. "Take your barn boots off, and sit yourself by the fire. Supper will be ready as soon as your father comes in."

Mason's stomach growled as he pulled the rocking chair closer to the stove.

"What are we having, Mama?" he asked.

"Chicken and biscuits and pumpkin pie," Mama sang out.

The door opened again and Father came in with a gust of the arctic air. Ice crystals laced his bushy eyebrows. Ira, Mason's four-year-old brother, raced across the room and Father caught him up in a bear hug.

Mama scurried to set the table, smiling now that her family was safe from the weather. To Mason, she always seemed to be in motion.

"Supper's all ready, Sterling," Mama said. "How is Chelsea?"

"That foal's coming tonight," Father said, setting Ira down. "Guess I won't be getting much sleep." He looked grave. "I'm more worried about this weather. I've never felt such cold, especially for so many days. The mercury's frozen in the thermometer. I figure it's close to fifty degrees below zero."

"Mercy!" said Mama. "As if things weren't bad enough with the war going on, and everyone short on fuel. I hope this new year will bring better times.''

They all sat at the table. Mama filled their plates with chicken and biscuits, which Father declared were the lightest in the county, then spooned on thick chicken gravy. Mason's mouth watered. He could hardly wait while Father said grace.

The first forkful of biscuit and gravy melted in his mouth. Mama did make the best biscuits.

''How was school today, Mason?'' Father asked.

''All right,'' Mason mumbled. He hurriedly took a bite of chicken and chewed vigorously. Mama wouldn't want him to talk with his mouth full.

School hadn't been all right. It had been awful. And it seemed to get worse every day because of Aden Cutler. Aden was much older, and bigger than Mason. He was in high school, but during recess some of the older boys always showed up at the grade school to bully the younger children. Aden was their ring leader, and he was meaner than anyone Mason had ever met.

It had been so cold in the schoolhouse that Miss MacKnight had let them huddle around the stove while they did their lessons. But the cold hadn't kept the boys from going outside, and the high school boys were there, waiting for them.

Aden had stolen his hat and filled it with snow. Then he'd pushed Mason down, sat on him, and jammed the snow-filled hat over Mason's head. Mason had felt like he was going to suffocate. He hadn't cried out, even when Aden punched him in the stomach, but tears had frozen to his cheeks and Aden had called him a baby. Worst of all, Aden had stolen his mittens, too, the red ones Mama had knit him for Christmas. It was small comfort that Aden was mean to everyone. He didn't pick fights with the high school boys; he tormented the younger children who weren't big enough or strong enough to fight back.

Anger flooded through him again, and the delicious supper turned to sawdust in his mouth. He finished his pumpkin pie without really tasting it, then excused himself. Mama and Father didn't notice when he left; they were discussing the food rationing. Europe was so far from Vermont, but the war there was affecting everyone's life.

Ira ran over to Mason, carrying a piece of paper.

"Look what I drew today," he said.

The paper was covered with squiggles and smudges.

"You can have it if you want," Ira said eagerly.

Mason pushed it away.

"I don't want it," he said. "It looks like a baby made it."

Ira's eyes filled with tears.

"Mason, is that any way to talk to your brother?" Father said sternly.

Mason looked at his feet.

"No, sir," he mumbled. "It's just . . ."

"Just what, son?"

"Nothing," Mason said. Father studied him for a moment, but didn't ask any more questions.

Mama cleared the table and put Ira to bed. Father worked by the stove, scraping an ax handle smooth with a piece of glass.

The clock struck nine and Father set down the handle.

"Guess I'll go check Chelsea again," he said. "Like to join me, son?"

Mason could hardly believe his ears.

"You mean I can stay up with you?" he asked. Even on Friday nights, Mama didn't let him stay up late.

Father chuckled.

"Well, the New Year is just a few days old, and you don't have school tomorrow. I figure helping that foal come into the world is as good a way as any to begin 1918."

"Be sure to dress warmly, Mason," Mama said quietly.

Mason put on his overcoat, hat, and boots, and thought he'd made it past his mother's sharp eyes.

"Where are your mittens?" Mama asked.

Mason's heart thudded.

"I lost them," he lied.

"Oh, Mason," Mama sighed. Mason braced himself for the scolding, but Mama just pressed her lips together. She went to the closet and brought out a pair of Father's old mittens.

"Wear these," she said. "You can't go out on a night like this without something on your hands." She smiled at him. Mason almost wished Mama had scolded him; he wouldn't have felt so guilty. And he hated Aden even more for making him feel that way.

The night seemed even colder now, after the comfort of the kitchen. The moisture from his breath turned to ice, and Mason felt icicles on his eyelashes. He was grateful when they reached the protection of the barn.

Chelsea was restless. Father spoke to the bay mare soothingly, and he and Mason sat just outside her stall on the edge of the lantern's light. Mason could hear the cows and Bennington, the other Morgan horse, munching hay. The wind howled outside, but the animals were safe and warm in the barn.

"You didn't lose your mittens, did you, Mason?" Father said quietly.

Mason didn't say anything for awhile. He just sat and breathed in the warm animal smells.

"Why do there have to be mean people?" he asked.

Father chewed thoughtfully on a piece of hay.

"That's a hard one to answer, son. Course now, if you were referring to one person in particular, there just might be an answer. Usually, they're angry at something, or someone, even themselves. Take that Aden Cutler, for example."

Mason sat up straight. Had Father read his mind? But Father went on talking without looking at him.

"I knew his father, George Cutler, before

19

he died. He was a cruel man, and drinking made him meaner. George beat his animals, and he didn't treat his family any better. His wife used to claim that she fell down the stairs, but she only seemed to fall down those stairs when George came home drunk. He beat Aden plenty, too, I imagine, just like he beat his cows. That boy got to believing he'd done something to deserve those beatings. Builds up anger, a desperation in a body. I expect Aden's lashing out at others 'cause he can't lash out at his father.''

Mason was trying to imagine what it would be like to live in a family like that when Father went on.

"I guess I don't have a good answer to your question, son. Your mother would say it takes all kinds of people to make a world. And some folks wonder how God could allow this war to happen."

"Mr. Watson says it's a glorious war."

"War's a terrible thing, son. It's not glorious, or manly, like so many say. It's pain and death and ruined lives. I think the glory is in watching the land produce something that wasn't there before you planted the seeds. Loving a good woman and raising fine children. There's glory in training a fine horse, like Bennington there, or being with your son in a warm barn on a cold night waiting for a new foal. Life's a miracle, son. I don't know why some folks are so eager to snuff it out.''

Mason settled deeper into the hay. Things were always all right when Father was around. If only he wouldn't have to go to school again and face Aden.

Mason thought he had closed his eyes just for a moment, but when Father shook his shoulder, the sky outside was pale where the sun would soon be rising.

''Wake up, son,'' Father said. ''The foal's coming.''

Chelsea lay on her side. Mason was frightened to hear her groaning and to see so much blood, but Father didn't seem to be alarmed. The foal's front legs and head

had emerged, wet and slick, looking shiny white through the sheath that held them. Chelsea groaned and heaved again, and the foal slid out onto the hay.

"It's a colt," Father said. "A bay."

Father peeled the bag and mucus from the foal's head. The foal twitched and Mason heard the quick intake of air as the colt took his first breath.

"Father," Mason ventured, "do you think I'm strong enough to help you train this colt?"

"Takes more than strength, son. It takes gentleness and patience to get the most out of a good horse."

Father doesn't think I can do it, Mason thought sadly, but his heart soared as Father continued.

"It will be awhile before this colt will be ready to train, but when it's time, you might be just the man I'm looking for to help me."

It was a fine way to start a new year.

TWO

School was no better the next week. On Monday, Aden stuffed snow into Mason's mouth. Mason flung himself at Aden, arms flailing, and got a bloody nose when Aden punched him in the face. On the second day, Aden took Mason's boots and threw them into Mr. Cleever's cow pasture.

"I wish you were dead!" Mason screamed. He was choking with rage. After his talk with Father, he'd started to feel sorry for Aden, but not anymore. If only I were bigger, he thought. I'd make Aden sorry he ever picked on me. He wouldn't ever dare touch me again.

Mason walked through the snow in his socks to retrieve his boots and was late for class. Miss MacKnight gave him a stern look. A few of the kids giggled. Mason slid into his seat, his face flushed as much with anger as shame. He sat all morning in wet socks, trying not to cry out from the pain as his feet thawed out. He wished Aden were dead. All afternoon, he dreamed of awful things he would do to get back at Aden.

The days dragged on. Mason dreaded going to school. The cold spell hung on, too. When the sun did shine, it seemed too weak to ever warm the earth again. In school, Miss MacKnight told them how glaciers once covered the land and carved the hills and valleys under mountains of ice. Mason wondered if this was the start of another Ice Age. If the glaciers came once, couldn't they come again? What if the snow never melted, and just kept piling up, year after year? Miss

MacKnight had also told them of the Year of No Summer, back in 1816. There was snow every month and no crops ripened, so people had left Vermont in droves. Maybe summer wouldn't come again. Mason tried to remember what the hills looked like when they were covered with new leaves, more green than anything could be, and the fields when Father turned the long black furrows with the heavy plow, killdeer crying and gliding over the rich, dark earth.

The cold made chores harder at home. The pump froze and Father and Mason hauled water in buckets from the river for the house and barn. Father chopped a hole through the ice on the river and said he had never seen the ice so thick. Just hauling water for the cows and horses kept Mason busy, for they drank a lot, but he had other chores to do, too. In the evenings, as he dragged the heavy pails and later fed the calves and forked down hay from the mow, he dreamed up reasons why he couldn't go to school the next day. When he woke in

the mornings, his stomach felt sick. One morning, he couldn't even eat breakfast.

"I'm not hungry, Mama," he said.

"Nonsense," she said. "Your brain needs fuel to learn. Besides, you're always hungry."

"I feel pretty sick, Mama. Maybe I shouldn't go to school."

"I declare, Mason, I don't know what's gotten in to you. Maybe you need a dose of castor oil."

Mason scurried out the door. Nothing was worse than castor oil. The thick slimy ball of it stuck in his throat for hours, no matter how much he swallowed.

He kicked at snow clumps in the yard. Maybe he could hide in the woods all day, then just go home at night. Maybe he could run away, go to live with his Aunt Margaret in Craftsbury. No, he didn't like Aunt Margaret, and besides, everyone would just call him a coward for running off like that. Maybe he could act like he'd slipped off the Black River bridge and pretend his leg was broken. Maybe it would be better to really have a broken leg than to have to be tormented by Aden.

Ira was in the yard. He held a stick in both hands, and he had Mama's tin colander on his head.

"What are you doing?" Mason asked him.

"I'm fighting the Germans," Ira said. "You'd better get down. They might shoot you."

"You look stupid," Mason said.

"Wanna play a little while?" Ira asked.

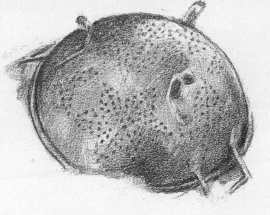

"You can wear my helmet and use my gun."

Mason cuffed Ira's head and knocked off the colander.

"Who'd want to play with you? You're just a dumb kid."

Ira's lips puckered, and he ran for the house.

"Crybaby, crybaby," Mason sang, but inside he wondered if he would ever feel worse than he did right then.

THREE

Father's birthday was coming.

Mason had been drawing a picture for him of Bennington and Chelsea pulling the big snow roller, with Father driving. He had worked on it for days, trying to make the horses look as real as he could. Miss MacKnight had praised it and held it up to show the rest of the class.

On the day before Father's birthday, Mason tucked the drawing carefully inside his coat and started for home.

It was a blustery day in late March. The sky was the color of Mama's pewter candlesticks. Snow devils swirled in the pasture along the road. Mason hoped there would be time to go sledding before chore time.

There was a lull in the wind as Mason got to the bridge over the river. He unbuttoned his coat and pulled out the drawing to admire it again. He was eager to show it to Father tomorrow.

A gust of wind plucked the picture from his mittened hand. It spiraled upward with the wind, then floated down, down, onto the ice of the Black River.

Mason couldn't believe it. His gift for Father had just been in his hand and now it lay hopelessly lost.

Maybe he could get it back. Maybe he could sneak out onto the river and grab the picture. It would just take a minute.

"Don't ever walk out onto that ice," Father had told him. "Ice that forms over running water isn't safe."

If he didn't go on the ice, his picture

would be carried away by the wind or swallowed by the river when the ice melted. Father would never see the work he had done.

Mason heard the snow crunch behind him. He looked over his shoulder and his heart sank. Aden stared at him, his blue wool hat pulled crookedly to one side.

"What are you crying about, kid?" Aden jeered.

Mason wiped his nose with his mitten.

"Nothing," he mumbled.

"Well, maybe I'll give you something to cry about," Aden said. He raised his fist.

A corner of the drawing fluttered in the wind, and the movement caught Aden's eye. He peered over the bridge railing.

"You draw that?" Aden asked.

Mason nodded miserably, waiting for Aden's punch.

"Who for?" Aden persisted.

"My father. Tomorrow's his birthday."

Aden dropped his fist. He stared at the paper on the river.

"Your father ever beat you?" he asked.

Mason was too stunned to answer. He shook his head dumbly.

"I seen your father working the horses once," Aden said. "He seemed real gentle with them. Didn't beat 'em or anything."

Before Mason could say anything, Aden slid down the riverbank and onto the ice.

The first crack of the ice sounded like a gunshot. Aden froze, his self-confident smile gone. Mason could hear the low-throated warning of the concealed water. Aden took another step and the ice cracked again.

Mason's stomach lurched. What would he do if Aden broke through? He could run to old Mrs. Rupert's house, but she wouldn't be able to help, and by the time he did find someone and get back to the river, he would be too late for Aden.

Aden lay on his belly and inched toward the picture. Mason could see drops of sweat on his pale forehead. He wanted to yell to Aden to come back, to forget about the picture, but he couldn't speak.

Aden reached the drawing, grabbed it, and turned around, still lying on his stomach. The ice cracked again, and Aden's nerve deserted him. He leaped to his feet and dashed for the riverbank. One foot broke through, and the cold black water surged over the ice. Mason moaned, and then Aden stood before him, flushed and breathing hard. He handed Mason the drawing.

"Don't tell anybody about this," was all he said. He pushed past Mason and ran up the road leading to the Cutler farm.

Mason stared at his drawing. He felt numb. He didn't even feel glad that Aden had saved his picture. He'd considered going onto that ice. If Father found out, he'd be furious. And he'd be even angrier to learn that Aden had risked his life just for a silly picture.

When Mason got home, he threw the drawing into his closet.

He was quiet at supper. Mama felt his forehead.

"Are you feeling all right, Mason?" she asked, but Mason only nodded. He did his chores and went to bed without being told.

The next morning, Mason gave the picture to Father. When Father said it was well done, Mason squirmed in his chair. He was afraid to tell Father about Aden and the ice, but he couldn't help feeling that the picture was more a present from Aden than from him.

That day at school, Aden didn't bother him at all.

FOUR

School was let out for sugaring season. Father drove Chelsea and Bennington through the woods and scattered the wooden buckets. Then he bored holes, one or two, in each maple tree. Mason hammered an iron spile into each hole, then he and Mama hung a bucket on each spile. As the sap dripped from the tree, it fell plunk, plunk into the bucket, a song of spring.

Father said sugaring depended on the weather; when the days were warm and the

nights dropped below freezing, then the sap ran best.

Father and Mason were in the woods every day now. They went from tree to tree, filling the gathering pails they carried with the clear, sweet sap, and poured it into the large wooden tub that Chelsea and Bennington pulled. Whenever Mason got thirsty, he drank cold sap from the buckets.

The snow was still deep in the woods. Father and Mason sank as they carried the pails to the tub. It was hard work, and Mason got tired, but he didn't complain. He felt proud to work with Father.

As he walked by one spruce tree, Mason chipped off a piece of the amber resin on the bark, and popped it into his mouth. He liked spruce gum's sharp flavor, but knew anything he ate later would taste terrible. Spruce gum's aftertaste didn't leave your mouth for a long time.

"It's the turpentine in it," Father had explained.

When the large tub was full, Father drove back to the sugarhouse. Mason liked these rides; they gave him a chance to rest, and there was something almost lulling about the thop, thop of the horses' hooves and the slosh of the sap in the tub. But he liked even better being in the sugarhouse.

There was so much to see, and smell, in the sugarhouse. The fire crackled and hissed in the arch, and thick clouds of fragrant steam billowed from the large flat pans that sat over the arch where the sap bubbled and boiled its way to syrup.

Mama boiled most of the syrup a little longer, then poured it into pails and tubs

where it crystallized. This was the family's sugar for the whole year. But Mama kept enough as syrup to use for pancakes and on oatmeal every morning.

Since sap is mostly water, it takes about forty gallons of sap to make one gallon of syrup. The water must be evaporated, or "boiled off." Father said boiling was an art, and he was proud of the way Mama boiled. She seemed to be everywhere: feeding wood into the huge iron arch to keep a steady, hot fire under the pans of boiling sap, watching the sap cook down, then drawing off the syrup when it reached the right density. The faster the sap was evaporated, the lighter in color and the higher its grade, so Mama boiled with only a shallow layer of sap in the pan, but watched closely. If the pans scorched, the syrup was spoiled.

Mama had never scorched the pans.

Mama put some of the hot syrup in a cup. Mason took a sip and let the delicate sweetness linger on his tongue.

"Leave a taste for me," Father said as he strode through the door.

"It's a good run, Geneva," he said. "The holding tank is full. Looks like a long night ahead."

"I shan't complain," Mama said. "We've needed more sugar, what with the rationing. If you'll take over, I'll run fix us some supper." She looked at Mason.

"If you'll pack a place in the snow, we'll have a special dessert."

"Sugar-on-snow!" Mason and Ira shouted together.

To Mason's stomach, it seemed like hours before Mama came back with their supper packed in an old apple box. Father turned over some wooden buckets for chairs, and they all sat around the arch. The light from the flames cast their shadows against the wall.

There were beans baked in syrup and hot corn bread. Mama had baked extra.

"I'm feeding two men now," she said and Mason felt warmth clear down to his toes.

"Me, too," said Ira.

"You're not a man," Mason said hotly.

"Am, too," Ira shouted, then laughed when Father swung him onto his shoulder.

"Before you two get to arguing, I'd like to get to my dessert," Father said and carried Ira and a kettle of syrup outside.

Mama had cooked some of the syrup down further and she ladled the syrup in swirls onto the snow where it cooled to a soft, waxy candy.

"Too bad we didn't have some pickles and doughnuts," Father joked.

Mama pulled back the dishcloth from the apple box. She lifted out a jar of pickles and a plate of golden doughnuts.

Father looked at Mama in amazement.

"Why, Geneva, when did you have time to make doughnuts?" he asked.

"Sugar-on-snow just wouldn't be the same without doughnuts," Mama said.

"You're a wonder," Father said quietly. Mama blushed, but Mason could tell she was pleased.

Mason ate the soft maple candy. Then he

ate a sour pickle to cut the sweetness so that he could eat more sugar-on-snow. And he ate five of Mama's sweet-milk doughnuts.

"We'll have to roll this boy to bed," Mama said and smiled.

It was a perfect evening. They were all together under the clear, cold sky. Mason felt full and sleepy, and content to just lean back against Father as the darkness deepened and settled like a sigh around them.

From the woods came a rasping noise.

"What's that sound?" Mason asked.

Mama, Father, and Ira listened, then Mama clapped her hands softly.

"It's a saw-whet owl," she said. "Oh, I haven't heard one in years."

"Listen to it," Father said to Mason, "and you'll hear how it got its name. Its call sounds like a man sharpening, or whetting, a large mill saw. It only makes the sound you hear in late winter, though."

They all listened.

"The first time I ever heard one was at this time of year when I was a little girl," Mama said. "My father went to filing one

of his saws, trying to coax the owl out, and before I knew it, that owl had flown in and landed on Papa's shoulder. Such a tiny thing. It could have fit in his hand." Mason saw the faraway look in her eyes. He tried to imagine her as a little girl.

"On a night like this, it's hard to believe there's a war going on and young men are dying," Father said. No one said anything for awhile.

"It is lovely out here," Mama sighed, "but I can't dawdle forever. We'll be here most of the night as is."

Mason and Ira got to stay in the sugar-house, too, on a made-up bed in the little loft. From his blankets, Mason could look out the square hole that served as a window.

The great dome of sky was speckled with stars. The Big Dipper was tipped over now, spilling onto Butternut Hill. Orion stood guard over the western horizon, and to the right of the Hunter, Mason found the fuzzy cluster of Pleiades, the Seven Sisters. He wondered if there were soldiers looking at the sky, too, watching the same stars he was and thinking of home.

Downstairs, Mama and Father took turns boiling. They sat talking, long into the night, their gentle voices rising with the steam, lulling Mason to sleep.

For three weeks, Mason and Father gathered the sap when it ran, and Mama kept busy boiling. The days grew warmer, and the snow melted from the woods, swelling the streams. The air was filled with the song of rushing water and the lonesome cries of geese winging north. When the trees began to bud, Father said sugaring was over.

Mason and Father picked up all the buckets from the woods and pulled the spiles from the trees. They took the buckets back to the sugarhouse and washed them, stacking them in preparation for next year.

School began again. Mason had been wondering if Aden had really changed or if the teasing would start all over again, but Aden didn't come to school the first day, or the next. When a week had gone by, Mason got up the courage to approach one of the other high-school boys.

"Where's Aden?" he asked.

"Didn't you hear? He ran off, joined the army."

Mason didn't know what to say. Did that mean Aden was never coming back to school?

The older boys started to talk among themselves. They were envious of what Aden had done.

"How could he enlist?" one of the boys asked. "He wasn't old enough."

"He went to Glover to join up 'cause around here they knew he was too young," said another. Mason knew him; he was Ed Hawkens, the storekeeper's son. "I'm going to join, too, soon's I can. With me and Aden over there, we'll send the Kaiser running with his tail between his legs." Ed hooted and started to wrestle with one of the other boys, and no one noticed when Mason slipped away. He wanted time to think. Aden wouldn't be bothering him anymore, but Mason didn't feel happy. Aden had been mean to him, but Mason hadn't stood up to him. Then Aden had saved the picture, but Mason hadn't thanked him. His stomach was so jumbled with emotion, he didn't know how he felt about Aden anymore.

He didn't know how he felt about himself.

FIVE

Mason was sure he loved spring the best: the smell of newly plowed earth, the blush of wildflowers in the pastures, the sweet perfume of apple blossoms, the flush of color, from gray to delicate green, that swept up the slope of Butternut Hill as the trees leafed out, and traipsing to the high pasture every day to check the ripeness of the wild strawberries. He was sure—until summer arrived and school was finished, and summer days that were his own stretched before him like a string of jewels. Anyway, he always liked to think of an endless string of days that were his own, but Father and Mama had different ideas about that than he did. There was always so much work to do on the farm, and Mason was old enough to help.

Mason and Mama planted the garden and kept it weeded. He, Father, and Mama hayed the fields together; Mama drove the horses, Father forked the hay up onto the wagon, and Mason stomped the hay down as Father had shown him so the load would hold together for the trip back to the barn. He helped Father lay new shingles on the back side of the barn, and on a rainy day, he and Mama wallpapered the living room. One day, Father sent Mason to whitewash the springhouse. Ira tagged along.

"Can I help, Mason?" Ira asked.

"Not here," said Mason, "but you think you're so big, you can feed the chickens. That will be your job now."

"Oh, boy," said Ira, clapping his hands.

Mason smiled wickedly.

"But there's something you'd better remember," he said. "Chickens will eat your toes. They'll bite them right off, if you let them near you." He knew he was being horrible, but he just couldn't seem to stop himself.

Ira's eyes opened wide.

"You backing out, crybaby?" Mason challenged.

Ira pressed his lips together.

"No," he said firmly, and ran to the barn to look at the chickens.

Most days held hard work, but there were fun times, too. After haying, they all went swimming in the spring-fed pond, where Mason liked to exhale and sink slowly into the cold depths of the water; he would close his eyes and feel the ropes of arum, arrowroot, and bullhead lily trail along his body. Other days, he, Ira, and Mama picked pails and pails of raspberries and blackberries, the dark, sweet juices staining their fingers. Once, Mason startled a bear in the thicket.

He stumbled through the bushes and almost fell on the furry black body. The bear woofed and spun around. Mashed berries stuck to the fur on his head. If Mason hadn't been so scared, he would have laughed at the bear's surprised expression. They stared at each other a few seconds, then the bear dropped to all fours and ran away faster than Mason would have thought an animal that size could run. Mason's knees shook a long time after the bear left.

Sometimes, Father could be talked into going fishing, usually on rainy days when other work couldn't be done. Mason wished he could fish alone with Father, but Ira always got to come along.

They fished the upper stretches of the Black River where it tumbled out of the hills and through the pasture where the horses grazed. It was fun to watch the colt, Jubal, race and buck and roll in the fragrant clover.

"You've been a great help to your Mother and me this year, Mason," Father said.

"Do you think I might be able to help

train Jubal to show him at the fair next year?" Mason asked, his heart thudding.

"Me, too," Ira cried.

Mason could have choked him.

"You're just a stupid baby," Mason muttered through clenched teeth. "Why do you always have to spoil everything?"

"Seems to me a boy that wants to train horses ought to be able to get along with his own brother," Father said quietly. Mason, his face flushed with shame and anger, knew better than to argue.

Summer passed too quickly. The routine of chores, school, and more chores resumed. Mason was surprised to find that he was almost the tallest in his class now, next to Gaston Lepage. He had grown over the summer without even realizing it, and he knew he was stronger. He was in the sixth grade now and sometimes when he had finished his sums, Miss MacKnight had him help the fifth grade with their spelling. Father and Mama were proud of his schoolwork, but Mason knew Father still thought of him as a boy too young to handle Jubal.

On a cloudless day in September, Father came back from town and searched out Mason.

"I feel like playing hooky," Father said. "It's a little early in the season yet, but let's make some cider." He tried to sound cheerful, but Mason thought his eyes looked sad.

Mason and Father piled baskets and feed sacks onto the wagon and Bennington pulled them up to the orchard on Butternut Hill. The old, gnarled trees held Greenings, Bethels, Duchess, and some crab apples that gave Father's cider a breezy tartness. A few of the trees were leafless, killed by the long cold spell of the winter.

"The Pumpkin Sweet's dead," Father said sadly. "My grandfather planted that tree." The Pumpkin Sweets were big yellow apples, as sweet as bananas. They were too sweet for Mason's taste, to eat right off the tree, but he and Father liked them baked and cut up into a bowl of bread and milk for Sunday supper.

Mason and Father carefully gathered several baskets of unblemished fruit that would be stored in the cellar just for eating and cooking. Father stored the best apples in hemlock sawdust to keep them crisp. Then Father sent Mason up the trees to shake down a hailstorm of the red and green globes.

From the branches, Mason faced the wind and looked toward the spine of the Green Mountains where the upper ridges were beginning to change color. There had already been several nights of frost, and it wouldn't be long before those ridges were covered with snow. The air was as crisp as the apples they gathered, and after their work, held the heavy sweetness of bruised fruit. Cradled in the arms of the tree, Mason wanted to reach out and hold the warmth in the earth just a little longer, to keep the season from spinning past so fast into winter.

Father was looking out over the valley, too. It was almost like he could hear Mason's thoughts.

"Seems like my bones feel the cold of

winter coming on earlier every year," Mason heard Father say. "I can feel the dying."

Mason wondered what dying Father was talking about: the fall flowers like aster and goldenrod, the soldiers, or his own, but Mason was afraid to ask.

Father drove the wagon to the barn and they unloaded the apples beside the huge oak press. Most farmers didn't have their own cider press and usually hauled wagonloads of apples to the cider mill in town, but Father had inherited both the large orchard and the oak press from his grandfather.

Father poured the feed sacks of apples, one at a time, through the grinder. There was a cylinder in the grinder which was studded with nails and as the cylinder turned, the nails chopped the apples into bits. Mason held Mama's washbasin under the cylinder to catch the pulp, or pomace as Father called it. Then it was time to put the pomace in the press, a large, slatted box that was too heavy for Mason to lift. Over the press there were two giant iron screws.

Mason poured several washbasins of pomace into the press and leveled it out with a hoe that Father had scrubbed clean. Father then spread a thick layer of clean oat straw over the pomace, and Mason put more apple pulp over the straw. He and Father kept layering the pulp and straw until the box was almost full.

Father laid a heavy plank over the straw and pomace, and turned the screws to press on the plank. Mason pushed a large wooden tub under the press; this was the part he liked best.

Father kept turning the screws, and as the plank pressed the pomace, the juice began to flow out into the tub, ruby-colored and fragrant.

"Nice, juicy apples," Father said. "Should give us a good yield."

When they were all done, they had thirty gallons of cider. Mason and Father each had a glassful and Mason thought it was the best-tasting cider he'd ever had, sweet and tart at the same time.

By the time he and Father had washed out the press, dusk had settled and the cows were waiting at the gate. Mason drove the cows into the barn and helped Father with the feeding and milking, then held the lantern while Father carried the full milk pails to the house.

They sat down to supper.

"I heard some news in town today," Father said as he stabbed a slice of ham. "Aden Cutler was killed in France."

Mason froze. Aden dead? Father continued.

"The telegram came to Mrs. Cutler this morning. Our troops had the Germans in full retreat. We were pushing them back through a place called the Argonne Forest. That's where Aden died."

They were all silent for a few moments, then Mama sighed.

"It's a terrible thing to say," she said, "but that boy was trouble, simple as that. I didn't wish bad for him, but he never did anything good his whole life."

Mama served up the scalloped potatoes.

She and Father began talking about poor Mrs. Cutler so no one heard Mason when he whispered, "Yes, he did."

That's why Father had looked sad when he came back from town, and why he had talked of dying. Why hadn't Father said anything to him while they were gathering apples, or pressing cider? All that time that Mason had been having fun, Aden had been dead.

Aden was in his dreams that night, images of Aden crawling on ice with Germans chasing him, firing rifles while he only had snowballs to throw at them. Aden broke through the ice and slipped under the dark water, while the Germans stood at the edge of the ice, firing their guns down into the jagged hole.

Mason woke, trembling and afraid to go back to sleep. What was it like to die? Aden had been so far from home and family. Mason tried to imagine what it would be like to be scared and all alone, not being able to see Father, Mama, or even Ira again. When he finally fell back into troubled sleep, he didn't hear Mama call and was late for school.

The whole school seemed subdued. The schoolyard was quiet even at recess. Aden hadn't been liked, but it was still a shock for the town to lose one of its own. No one was able to concentrate and, for the first time ever, Miss MacKnight sent everyone home early.

Mason didn't feel like playing, and went to the barn to do his chores. Ira was feeding the chickens and Mason stood in the shadows to watch him. Ira held the pan of corn in one hand, his other hand on the door. The chickens raced over to be fed, and Ira jumped backward, spilling the corn on the ground. His face was white.

He's scared of them! Mason thought with surprise. Because of what I told him. And he realized with shame that he'd been as mean to Ira as Aden had ever been to him. Ira probably hated him. Maybe Ira wanted him dead, just like he'd wanted Aden dead.

Only I didn't really want him to die, thought Mason.

Mason put a hand on Ira's shoulder. Ira jumped again.

"I used to be afraid of chickens," Mason said.

"You were?" Ira said. He stared up at Mason, his eyes huge.

"Sure," said Mason. "The trick is not letting them know you're afraid. You just walk in there and pretend to be brave. Follow me."

He would talk with Father tonight, and tell him all about being mean to Ira. He could have helped Ira this summer, he could have taught him to swim, showed him which pools the largest brook trout liked to hide in, played catch with him. He would start being a better brother. And tonight, he would tell Father about Aden saving the picture, and Father would know that Aden Cutler had done at least one good thing in his life.

Mason got a new pan of corn and they

walked together into the pen. Ira clung to him like a shadow, but instead of being annoyed, Mason felt stronger and happier than he had for a long time.

SIX

M ason, Ira, and Mama were stacking the last of the firewood. That noon, Mama had sent Father to town.

"You've been working so hard, Sterling," she said. "Give yourself a rest. Mason and I can finish the wood."

It was a clear day but cold. Mason breathed on his hands to warm them. The crows were flocking, and a chorus of their raspy cawing rose from the cornfield.

Over the past few weeks, Mason, Father,

and Mama had dug the potatoes, carrots, turnips, and beets and stored them in the cellar. He and Father had picked sacks of butternuts. Later, on winter nights, he and Father would break their hard shells and Mama would use the rich nut meats in cakes and maple candy. Father had brought a wagonload of fir boughs from the woods, and he and Mason had piled them around the outside of the house to help keep out the winter cold. Mason and Mama had held the heavy storm windows, while Father latched them in place. All of them felt ready for winter.

Movement on the road caught Mason's eye. It was Father coming back from town. Father was leaning low over Chelsea, running her flat out. Mason felt the hair stand up on his neck.

Mama was beside Mason in an instant, shading her eyes.

"Something's wrong," she said. "Sterling never runs that horse."

Father clattered into the yard and slid off Chelsea's back.

"The war is over!" he shouted. "The war is over!"

He grabbed Mama by the waist and whirled her around. Sometimes when he did this, Mama would push against him, saying, "Oh, Sterling, put me down," but when Mason looked at them, twirling in the afternoon sun, Mama was hugging Father, and her eyes were shining through her tears.

"Is it really over, Father?"

Father caught Mason up in his embrace.

"Yes, son. The killing's over. And the men will be coming back."

Not all the men, thought Mason. Not Aden.

The years seemed to melt from Father and he laughed like a boy.

"Go get the sleigh bells from the barn, son. And the cowbell, too. Hurry. Everyone in town's meeting at the church. Every bell we have will ring tonight."

Mason ran for the bells, while Father rubbed Chelsea down and put her in the stable. Then he helped Father hitch Bennington to the buggy. Mason felt feverish with excitement. He'd never seen Father so giddy.

They all clambered into the buggy. Father looped the sleigh bells around his neck and clucked twice. Bennington stretched into his road trot, his black hooves flashing, eating up the miles. Mama clutched her hat, and never once suggested to Father that he should slow down.

They heard the shouts from town long before they got there. Father was right, Mason thought. Everyone in town must have showed up; the street was crowded with people and horses.

"What's that line for?" Mason asked, pointing toward the church.

"The men are taking turns ringing the church bell. Why don't you come get in line with me?"

Mason's heart swelled. The men, Father had said.

"Okay," Mason said. "But I gotta do something first."

Mason hadn't realized he was searching the crowd for a face until he saw her, Mrs. Cutler, standing by the town hall a little apart from the crowd. Her arms were wrapped around her chest as if she was hugging herself. She looked old and sad.

"Mrs. Cutler?"

She turned and Mason felt panic. What could he say to her?

"It's about Aden," he stammered.

"Aden's dead," she said flatly. "Probably you're glad about that. Seems most folks are. Oh, they don't say that, but I can tell what they're thinking."

"No, ma'am, I'm not glad."

She didn't seem to have heard him.

"That boy, he was a handful. Has been ever since his daddy died. I know people thought he was worthless, but he wasn't so bad as folks say."

"I know," said Mason. "He did something for me once and I never thanked him. I wish he were coming back." Then he wished he hadn't said that; Mrs. Cutler's lower lip began to tremble.

"I'm sorry," Mason said, and turned to leave.

"Thank you," she said. "Nobody ever said anything nice about my boy before."

Father was calling, and Mason couldn't

think of anything else to say. He left Mrs. Cutler and ran to get in line. But he'd already decided. Tomorrow he would go over to Mrs. Cutler's and split and pile her wood for winter. She'd be needing some help around the farm now.

When his turn came, Mason grabbed the rope and pulled with all his strength. The first peal of the bell rang out like a rifleshot.

From the surrounding hills answered the voices of other bells. The air was so clear, bells could be heard from towns as far as fifteen miles away, their sweet crystal notes like birdsong.

In the church, the women had filled the tables with coffee and doughnuts and the men were lined up, whooping and drumming each other on the back, waiting for their turn to pull the rope. The bells would ring all night.

In the gathering dusk, Mason pulled the rope, ringing for peace and lost innocence, ringing the bell for Aden.

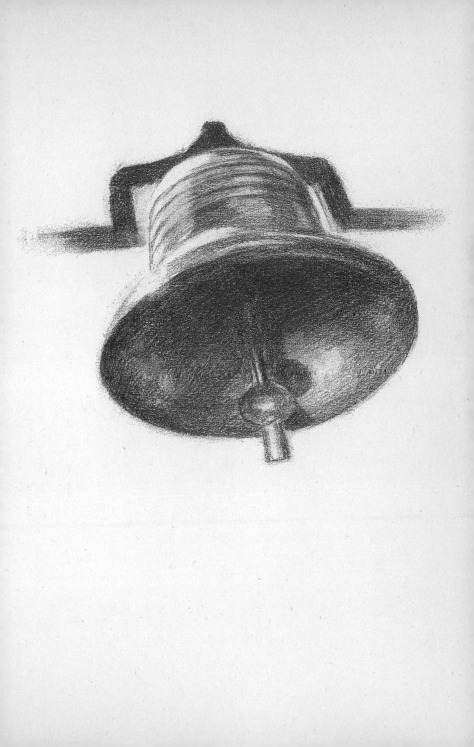

Natalie Kinsey-Warnock grew up on a farm in Vermont. An avid athlete, artist, and writer, she finds her inspiration in the northern hills there, where she lives with her husband, Tom.

She is the author of *The Canada Geese Quilt*, *Sweet Memories Still*, and other children's books.

Leslie W. Bowman lives in Minneapolis, Minnesota. She has illustrated a number of children's books, including *The Canada Geese Quilt*.

OTHER PUFFIN CHAPTERS YOU MAY ENJOY